SPOOKY
GORGONZOLA'S REVENGE

SUNNYSIDE
PRIMARY SCHOOL

Collins
RED
STORYBOOK

First published in Great Britain
by CollinsChildren'sBooks in 1995
3 5 7 9 8 6 4 2

CollinsChildren'sBooks is a division of HarperCollins*Publishers*
Ltd, 77-85 Fulham Palace Road, London W6 8JB

Text copyright © Karen Wallace 1995
Illustrations copyright © Judy Brown 1995

The author and artist assert the moral right to be identified as
the author and artist of the work.

Printed and bound in Great Britain by Caledonian
International Book Manufacturing Ltd, Glasgow G64

0 00 674896 1

GORGONZOLA'S REVENGE

by Karen Wallace
Illustrated by Judy Brown

CollinsChildren'sBooks
An Imprint of HarperCollinsPublishers

TO MRS ROMYN,
WITH LOVE

Chapter One

A mouse called Gorgonzola stretched out in front of a hot stove. It was a good life for a mouse. Every night Granny Flanagan sat in the same rocking chair, read the same newspaper and dropped lots of biscuit crumbs.

And best of all, cats made Granny Flanagan sneeze.

Gorgonzola rolled over to warm her fat furry stomach. Perhaps one more mouthful...

"Gorgonzola!" squeaked a voice. "Wake up!"

Gorgonzola opened her eyes. A mouse called Crackers was staring at her. "Your paw was going in and out of your mouth," he said. "I thought you were going to bite it off."

"I was dreaming my favourite dream," murmured Gorgonzola. "In the old days before…" her voice tailed away.

Across the room the rocking chair was empty but the same newspaper lay on the floor. Gorgonzola gazed at the front page; October 29th 1894 was printed on the top left hand corner.

Gorgonzola was over a hundred years old. Gorgonzola was a ghost mouse. She was shiny and silvery and shone like a teaspoon. She was also the head of the family and all the other ghost mice looked up to her.

"I know about Granny Flanagan," said Crackers, Gorgonzola's great-great-grandson. "She read the old newspaper and went to the Big Cheese Shop in the sky."

Gorgonzola smiled. "That's right," she said, "and we've looked after Honeycomb Cottage ever since." Gorgonzola believed that ghosts should have a keen interest in their own history and ghost mice were no exception.

"Do you think we'll stay forever?" asked Crackers, with a hopeful look on his face.

"Of course we will," said Gorgonzola. "We'll never leave Honeycomb Cottage."

But at that very moment a mouse called Porridge Oats stumbled through the wall into the room, his whiskers shaking and his beady eyes rolling wildly in his head.

"What on earth's the matter," cried Gorgonzola.

"Strangers!" gasped Porridge Oats. "There are strangers walking up the path and one of them's got the big key!" Gorgonzola had just turned to look out of the window when they heard an unmistakable rattle and the big key turned in the front door lock.

Chapter Two

Melanie Murdock strode into the kitchen at Honeycomb Cottage. She was wearing a fake fur cape with matching scarlet leggings and heavy gold jewellery jangled at her neck and wrists.

Gorgonzola and Porridge Oats gasped as she wiped her pink-booted foot all over the precious old newspaper in front of the stove.

"It's just as I thought," said Melanie Murdock, her hard green eyes flicking around the room.

Behind her, Simon Slime of Slime & Slime Estate Agents, rubbed his hands.

"Yes," he murmured. "Superbly untouched. A rustic jewel with," he pulled open a shutter, "stunning views over – eugh." Melanie Murdock jabbed him with the umbrella she wore like a sword around her waist.

"Don't interrupt," she said. "This place is a dump. Everything needs changing." She waved a jewelled hand in the air. "I see arches, patios, huge french windows."

"Don't forget the kitchen, sweetest," said Hugo Murdock from underneath a fluffy golfing cap. He bent down to Simon Slime who was lying on the floor, clutching his stomach. "Melanie is an interior designer, you know," he whispered.

"I shall have every gadget!" said Melanie Murdock, her eyes spinning like tops. "They shall be push-button, sterilised, and beige. There is no place for clutter or colour in my kitchen." She whacked the stove with her umbrella. "And that will go first."

In the darkness of her hole, Gorgonzola's heart was sinking faster than a turnip in a pond.

"I was hoping the stove would be lit again," she whispered to Porridge Oats. "It was always so nice and warm behind it."

"I don't think anything is going to be nice and warm again," said Porridge Oats in a low voice.

"And one more thing," said Melanie Murdock, waving her umbrella menacingly.

Simon Slime covered his face. "What's that?" he muttered.

"Sniff!" said Melanie.

"I beg your pardon?" said Simon
Slime.

"I said SNIFF," commanded Melanie.
She turned to her husband. "You too,
Hugo."

Hugo sniffed. Simon Slime sniffed.

"Well?" said Melanie. Her hand
hovered over her umbrella handle.
"Can you smell it?"

Hugo looked at Simon Slime.

Simon Slime looked at Hugo.

The window was open. Soft spring air
filled the room. "Flowers?" said
Simon Slime.

"Pine needles?" said Hugo.

"Mice," said Melanie Murdock in a
low, dangerous voice, and she emptied
her bag on to the table.

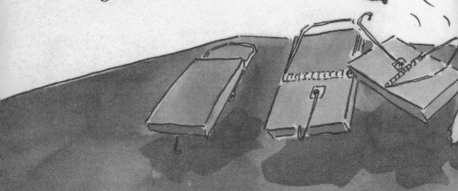

Hugo and Simon stared at a lump of mouldy cheese and half-a-dozen bits of wood stuck with wires. Melanie Murdock pressed her scarlet lips together.

"That should do the trick," she said.

The mice watched in amazement as Simon Slime and Hugo cut a lump of cheese into tiny pieces and stuck bits onto the wires.

"Perhaps they're trying to be nice to us, after all," said Pudding Rice, remembering how much he used to like cheese.

Gorgonzola shook her head. "Those things are mousetraps," she said. "They can't hurt us now we're ghosts, but they're bad news all the same."

Pudding Rice looked puzzled. "Why?" he asked.

"Only nasty people put down traps," explained Gorgonzola. "Not the sort of people who should live in Honeycomb Cottage."

"All sorted, sweetest," said Hugo, as he put the last trap down in front of the larder. "What shall we do now?"

Melanie opened the front door. "Come back later," she said with a nasty smile.

"The strangers don't like us!" wailed a mouse called Cheesestraw. But Gorgonzola merely turned the mousetraps towards the window, picked up a twig and poked them.

BANG! BANG! BANG! Bits of cheese shot through the air and into the garden.

"Never forget," said Gorgonzola, with a determined look in her eye. "We were here first and we've been here for a very, very long time."

Chapter Three

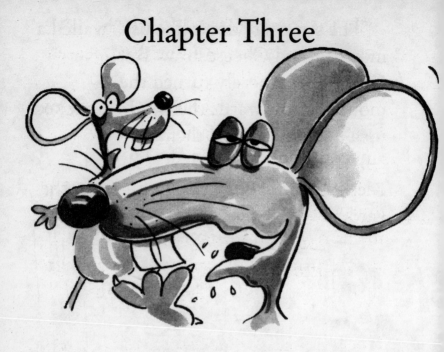

"Gorgonzola!" squeaked Crackers.
"Wake up! There's something funny
going on!"

Gorgonzola opened her eyes. "Why is
it so black?" she whispered.

"The strangers came back," said
Crackers. "They blocked up our holes."

"How dare they?" squeaked
Gorgonzola, "Where are the others?"

"In the kitchen," said Crackers, "waiting for you." And he disappeared through the wall.

In the kitchen it was bright and sunny. Pudding Rice was staring at a new supermarket leaflet. He had been a greedy mouse even before he became a ghost and now he passed the time memorizing all the fancy labels and special offers that were stuffed through the letterbox. The others were busy dusting off the precious old newspaper. Gorgonzola felt her heart swell in her chest. This was how Honeycomb Cottage had always been and this was how it should stay.

"We'll give them one last chance," she said as a car door slammed outside and the big key turned in the lock. "Then we'll decide."

"Check the traps," called Melanie. "I'll bring the shopping."

Hugo Murdock, wearing tartan dungarees and a pale yellow beret, walked into the kitchen. He peered at the mousetraps.

No cheese. No mice.

"Simon Slime must have been here," he said to himself as he dumped what he was carrying on to the firewood pile.

Gorgonzola gasped. It was the old Honeycomb Cottage sign.

"Well?" said Melanie, sniffing in a meaningful way as she walked into the kitchen.

"All gone, sweetest," said Hugo.

"Good riddance," said Melanie, as she put an armful of supermarket bags on the table.

"I have a surprise for you, sweetest," said Hugo, and he handed her a long, brown paper parcel.

Melanie ripped it open. Inside was a green plastic sign with the words HUGMEL HOUSE stamped in gold across it.

"It's your name and my name and the name of our new house," croaked Hugo with a soppy smile.

A cold fury rose in Gorgonzola's chest as Melanie planted a shiny red lipstick mark on Hugo's blotchy cheek.

"And I've got a surprise for *you*," she cried triumphantly, and unrolled a big piece of paper and stuck it to the wall like a map. "My plans!"

The word sent a shiver through every mouse in the room. One by one they moved up closer to get a better look.

On the wall was a picture of a house that didn't look anything like Honeycomb Cottage. There were arches and french windows everywhere. The garden had been concreted over and covered in Melanie's collection of stone dachshunds and plastic cactuses and in the middle of the garden, instead of Granny Flanagan's lily pond, was a large fountain in the shape of a power drill.

"Where's my miniature golf course supposed to go?" asked Hugo in a wounded voice.

"In the flower garden," cooed Melanie sounding like a vulture with a sore throat. "I chose it for you specially. It's very sunny there and the soil is excellent."

"That's a good idea," said Hugo. "It will be easy to dig all those holes."

"Exactly," replied Melanie. "Now help me empty the car. There's lots to do before the bulldozers come."

"What are bulldozers?" said Gorgonzola.

It wasn't only Pudding Rice who read the leaflets from the superstore. Porridge Oats liked the DIY section.

"They're big, yellow monsters," he said slowly. "And they knock down walls."

Something snapped in Gorgonzola's head and she ran to the arm of the rocking chair. "Emergency meeting!" she squeaked, and a second later every mouse in the cottage was sitting on the seat of the chair looking up at her.

"These strangers want big, yellow monsters to destroy Honeycomb Cottage," said Gorgonzola, her voice harsh with rage. "We've got to get rid of them!" Then she squeezed her eyes tight and held on to her whiskers with both paws.

"We'll never do it," wailed a young mouse, clutching at Gorgonzola's tail.

"Ssh," hissed Porridge Oats. "Gorgonzola's thinking."

When Gorgonzola opened her eyes there was a big smile on her face. "I've got it!" she cried. "We're ghosts, aren't we? We'll haunt them!" She paused remembering Melanie Murdock's own words. "That should do the trick!"

Porridge Oats clapped his paws in excitement. "Brilliant!" he cried. "We'll treat them just like they treated us!"

"Where shall we set the first trap?" said Gorgonzola.

"What about in front of the larder?" suggested Pudding Rice with a chortle.

Chapter Four

That night Hugo Murdock couldn't sleep. He tried thinking happy thoughts, like how fast his power drill would put holes in the cottage walls, or how efficiently his circular saw would slice through the old beams in the kitchen, but nothing worked. Beside him, Melanie snored and made jabbing movements with an imaginary umbrella. Finally, Hugo sat up and looked around him. Even though it was pitch black, the room seemed to be full of tiny eyes staring at him.

There's something peculiar about
this cottage, thought Hugo. It's
almost as though it doesn't like us.
Then he shook his head and told
himself he was imagining things,
but that was peculiar too,
because Melanie had told him
time and time again that he
had no imagination.
"What I need is a glass
of milk and a biscuit,"
said Hugo out loud.
He put on his dressing
gown with Heavyweight
Hugo embroidered on
the back and went
downstairs to
the kitchen.

The white door of the larder gleamed faintly. Hugo stepped forward to open it.

SNAP! He let out a howl as a terrible pain shot across the big toe of his right foot.

"What's all that noise?" cried Melanie from the top of the stairs.

"Did you put a mousetrap in front of the larder?" asked Hugo, rubbing at his red, swollen toe.

"Of course I didn't," said Melanie. "There aren't any mice, remember?"

The next morning Hugo woke late, in a bad mood with a sore toe and a headache.

In the kitchen, Melanie was furious. She had got up early to disinfect the supermarket tins before putting them away and found the table covered in cereal.

"Mucky pup," she muttered.

"Who's a mucky pup?" said Hugo coming into the kitchen.

"You are," said Melanie. "Leaving cereal all over the table last night."

"I didn't touch the cereal," said Hugo, sitting down and opening *Drill Bits*, his favourite magazine. Then his jaw dropped open. A row of mouse-shaped paper dollies had been chewed out of the inside pages.

"Why did you cut up my magazine?" he asked slowly.

Melanie put down the tin she was wiping and stared at him. "I haven't touched your magazine," she said icily.

"Then it must be mice," said Hugo.

"There-aren't-any-mice," said Melanie, spitting out each word. "We haven't seen any and you told me yourself the traps were empty. Anyway, why would a mouse go to the trouble of chewing mouse-shaped paper dollies in your favourite magazine?"

Hugo shook his head. Put like that it did sound rather unlikely, but then who did do it? Underneath the table, his sore toe began to throb. And who put the trap near the larder? He found himself looking suspiciously at Melanie again.

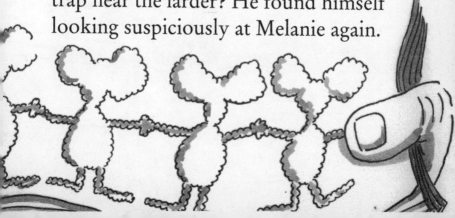

On top of the fridge, Gorgonzola started to giggle. Soon all the mice were rolling about holding their shiny stomachs and laughing their heads off. They made a high silvery sound a bit like tiny bells jingling.

Melanie Murdock turned and stared at Hugo. "What was that?" she said.

"Birds," muttered Hugo.

Chapter Five

After breakfast Hugo pinned his toy measuring tape on to his tartan dungarees and went out to dig up the rose garden. When he came in at lunch time, Melanie was reading a piece of paper she had found in the letter box.

"Darling," she said with her sharp-toothed smile. "There's a cake decorating competition in the village hall tomorrow. I thought I might enter and meet some of the weirdos that live around here."

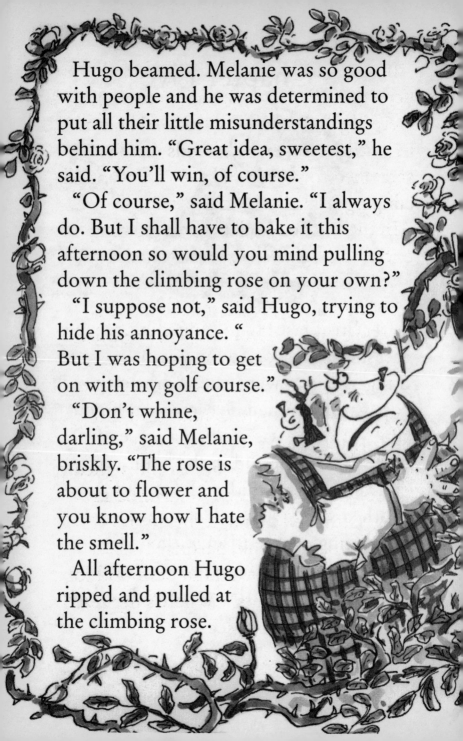

Hugo beamed. Melanie was so good with people and he was determined to put all their little misunderstandings behind him. "Great idea, sweetest," he said. "You'll win, of course."

"Of course," said Melanie. "I always do. But I shall have to bake it this afternoon so would you mind pulling down the climbing rose on your own?"

"I suppose not," said Hugo, trying to hide his annoyance. " But I was hoping to get on with my golf course."

"Don't whine, darling," said Melanie, briskly. "The rose is about to flower and you know how I hate the smell."

All afternoon Hugo ripped and pulled at the climbing rose.

It was a difficult job. The rose had been there a long time and its thorns were big and sharp. By teatime, he was in a filthy temper. His hands were scratched to shreds and the rose was still clinging stubbornly to the wall.

In the kitchen Melanie was gloating over the cake she had just created. It was heart-shaped, decorated with ribbons and rosebuds and on the top was a beautiful silver stagecoach pulled by four white mice. Inside the coach a princess with champagne-coloured hair, just like Melanie's, was holding a tiny gold whip.

Melanie clasped her hands and sighed. "It's my best ever," she murmured as Hugo stumped through the door. "What do you think, darling?"

Hugo was hungry and in no mood for paying compliments. "Where's my tea?" he asked in a sour voice.

Melanie glared at him. "The same place as your power tools," she snapped. "In the cupboard."

Hugo bandaged his hand and opened the cupboard door.

"What's he doing now?" whispered Gorgonzola from inside the box of power tools.

"Getting some biscuits," said Porridge Oats who was keeping a look out from the top shelf. "You have a few more minutes yet."

"We'll be ready," whispered Crackers.

Ten minutes later Hugo put down his mug of tea and lifted the power saw from its box. It was difficult to hold with his bandaged hand, but Hugo didn't mind. Sawing things up – it didn't matter what – was one of his favourite hobbies. He rested the blade against an old oak beam and pushed the start button.

Nothing happened.

Below him Melanie was humming tunelessly and fiddling with an icing bag.

"Darling," said Hugo as sweetly as he could manage. "My drill's not working."

Melanie put down her icing bag. "Can't you do anything properly?" she muttered.

Hugo ignored her and pressed the button again. Nothing happened.

He turned the drill upside down. The cable was broken! Melanie must have caught it in the cupboard door when she put the tools away.

"Melanie," he bawled, suddenly losing his temper. "You broke the cable."

He stumped down the ladder and looked in his box. "You've broken the cables on all my tools."

Melanie stared at him with her weed-coloured eyes.

"Don't be ridiculous, Hugo," she said. "I never touched your tools."

"Well, somebody has," said Hugo, "and it can't have been mi…" He never finished his sentence. In his ears he heard again the high silvery sound and now it seemed to be coming from inside the cupboard. A prickly feeling crept over him. Hugo found himself shivering even though it was warm in the kitchen.

"Melanie," he said in a different voice. "Have you noticed anything, um, peculiar, about this cottage?"

Melanie looked at him as if he was mad. "The only peculiar thing I've noticed is the way you are behaving," she said, and turned back to her cake.

In the cupboard Gorgonzola wrapped her paws around her body and hugged herself. "It's working!" she cried, her sharp teeth glittering in the dark. "We're winning!"

"I should think so too," said Pudding Rice, who had just crept in beside her. "Have you seen the cake she's made?" And he described it in minute detail down to the exact length of the tiny gold whip.

Gorgonzola could feel herself go hot under her fur.

"Did you say four MICE were pulling the carriage?" she spluttered.

Pudding Rice nodded slowly.

"Don't forget the gold whip," squeaked Crackers.

For a moment Gorgonzola was too angry to speak, then she pulled herself up to her full height and puffed out her chest. "These strangers have heaped insult on injury," she declared.

"Here here," said a mouse.

"Sshh," said another.

Gorgonzola took a deep breath. "We shall leave no stone unturned. We will show no mercy," she cried. "They will wish they had never set eyes on our cottage."

Later that evening Melanie banged two cups of watery cocoa on the table.

"I've been thinking about what you said," she muttered. "Maybe there is something peculiar going on. Anyway, I think we should lock ourselves in tonight."

"Good idea," said Hugo, and he walked over to where the key was supposed to be. But the key wasn't there and the ribbon it usually hung from was ripped in half.

"It's probably fallen down behind the chest of drawers," said Melanie taking a large slurp of cocoa.

Hugo bent down and felt underneath. SNAP! He yowled and pulled back his hand. A mousetrap was swinging from his bandaged thumb!

Behind him there was a low choking sound and Hugo looked up to see Melanie rocking backwards and forwards, holding her hand over her mouth and sobbing with laughter. "You did that on purpose," he yelped, his face purple with rage.

"I didn't! I didn't!" cried Melanie, tears pouring down her cheeks. "I didn't touch anything!"

Chapter Six

"I'm sorry I laughed at you," said
Melanie, as she climbed into bed. "I
couldn't help it.   Something about this
house is giving me the jitters."

Hugo tried to pat her arm with his
doubly-bandaged hand but it hurt too
much. "I know what you mean," he
muttered. "I keep thinking I'm being
watched."

"I keep hearing things," said Melanie.
"The problem is," she said slowly, "if I
didn't know better, I'd swear it was
mice."

Hugo thought of the tiny bright eyes and the strange silvery laughter. "Maybe the place is haunted," he said. "Some old cottages are, you know."

"But nobody has lived here for a hundred years," said Melanie.

"Except a whole lot of mice," said Hugo in a hollow voice.

"There's no such thing as ghost mice," said Melanie, blowing out the candle. "Let's go to sleep. The cake competition's in the morning and the bulldozers are coming."

Two minutes later she was snoring like a pig full of custard.

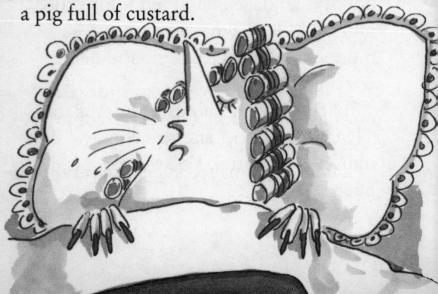

"Did you hear that?" whispered Crackers.

Cheesestraw nodded. "We'd better tell Gorgonzola."

Gorgonzola called an immediate meeting on the rocking chair.

"They've got to go by tomorrow morning," she said. "Or Honeycomb Cottage will be destroyed."

There was a shocked silence. Everybody was thinking hard.

"I've got an idea," said Porridge Oats.
"I've got one too," said Pudding Rice.
"They'd better be good," warned
Gorgonzola. "This is our last chance."
Porridge Oats and Pudding Rice
climbed onto the arm of the chair and
whispered in Gorgonzola's ears. As they
spoke a huge smile spread across her
face and when they finished,
Gorgonzola stood up.
"I think we've done it!" she cried,
slapping her thigh with glee.

Chapter Seven

"Hugo!" said Melanie, shaking him.
"Wake up! Something horrible's
happened."

Hugo opened his eyes. It was pitch
black. "What's the time?" he muttered.

"It's nine o'clock in the morning," said
Melanie.

"Nine o'clock?" said Hugo. "Why is
it so dark?"

"Because the window has been blocked up," said Melanie in a strangled voice.

Hugo put on his dungarees and stumbled downstairs to the kitchen. He yanked back the shutters. The window was blocked up. Every window in the house was blocked up!

Hugo turned the handle on the front door and pushed. The door was locked, but how? A cold, sick feeling crept across his stomach. Suddenly there was an ear-splitting scream behind him and he turned to see Melanie standing in the larder, shining a torch at her cake. Except that the thing in the torch beam wasn't the cake she had made. Hugo gasped with horror.

Melanie's cake had been chewed to form a circular platform. The stagecoach and the princess had disappeared and in the middle of the platform was a huge mouse made out of icing sugar. Its head was thrown back, its whiskers were rigid, its muscles were flexed like a superhero. It had the look of a mouse

who had won a great battle.

"Hugo," croaked Melanie. "Do you remember what you said last night?"

Hugo nodded and led her slowly into the kitchen. He shut the door on the terrible figure made of icing sugar and made her sit down on a chair.

Melanie's face was grey as a wasp's nest. A horrible realisation was creeping over her. She thought of the mousetrap in front of the larder, and the one under the chest of drawers. She thought of the mouse-shapes chewed in Hugo's magazine, and last of all she thought of the monster on top of her cake.

"Hugo," croaked Melanie. "I think you're right. I think this cottage is haunted."

"By mice?" whispered Hugo.

"By mice," whispered Melanie.

They sat in silence staring at each other.

You could have heard a biscuit crumble, said Gorgonzola afterwards.

"Hugo?" whispered Melanie again.
"Yes, dear?"

"Yes dear," said Hugo as calmly as he could. "The problem is we're, um, blocked in."

"Blocked in! Blocked in!" yelled Melanie. "I won't be blocked in to my own cottage like some, some…"

"Mouse?" said Hugo hopelessly.

Melanie's eyes whirled round like soup plates at a circus. She picked up a hammer and smashed it against the front door.

"Come in," said Simon Slime in a silly voice. "I mean, can I come in?"

For a second neither Hugo or Melanie could believe their ears. Then Melanie whacked the door again.

"Come in!" said Simon Slime again. "Or perhaps I should say 'knock knock!'"

There was a high-pitched titter.

"Let me out you idiot," yelled Melanie Murdock.

Simon Slime looked down. The big key was lying on the doorstep at his feet. He shrugged and opened the door.

Bright light burst into the darkened room.

"I say," sniggered Simon Slime. "It's rather like a mouse hole in here."

"It IS a mouse hole," shouted Melanie.

"And it's haunted!" She picked up her handbag. "We're leaving and we're never coming back!"

Hugo gathered up his tools. "Melanie's plans are ruined," he told Simon Slime "So are my tools. The ghost mice did it."

"Ghost mice?" said Simon Slime, staring at him as if he had gone completely mad. Come to think of it, they both looked completely mad. He opened his mouth to say something soothing but before he could speak, the door slammed shut.

Melanie and Hugo Murdock were gone.

Simon Slime looked around the kitchen. Nothing much seemed to have changed. There was even an old newspaper still lying on the floor. He knocked out the boards blocking the window, then he picked up the Honeycomb Cottage sign.

"He's putting it back," cried Gorgonzola. "Honeycomb Cottage is ours again."

A great cheer went up! There was a drumming of feet and a waving of paws in the air.

Simon Slime shivered as he turned the big key in the lock. A most peculiar sound was coming from inside the old cottage. It was high and silvery like the jingling of little bells. It fluttered in the air like the beating of tiny wings. It was the sound of ghost mice laughing and dancing. It was the sound of Honeycomb Cottage, happy once more.